Dear Parents:

Congratulations! Your child is taking the first steps on an exciting journey. The destination? Independent reading!

STEP INTO READING® will help your child get there. The program offers five steps to reading success. Each step includes fun stories and colorful art or photographs. In addition to original fiction and books with favorite characters, there are Step into Reading Non-Fiction Readers, Phonics Readers and Boxed Sets, Sticker Readers, and Comic Readers—a complete literacy program with something to interest every child.

Learning to Read, Step by Step!

Ready to Read   Preschool–Kindergarten
• big type and easy words • rhyme and rhythm • picture clues
For children who know the alphabet and are eager to begin reading.

Reading with Help   Preschool–Grade 1
• basic vocabulary • short sentences • simple stories
For children who recognize familiar words and sound out new words with help.

Reading on Your Own   Grades 1–3
• engaging characters • easy-to-follow plots • popular topics
For children who are ready to read on their own.

Reading Paragraphs   Grades 2–3
• challenging vocabulary • short paragraphs • exciting stories
For newly independent readers who read simple sentences with confidence.

Ready for Chapters   Grades 2–4
• chapters • longer paragraphs • full-color art
For children who want to take the plunge into chapter books but still like colorful pictures.

STEP INTO READING® is designed to give every child a successful reading experience. The grade levels are only guides; children will progress through the steps at their own speed, developing confidence in their reading.

Remember, a lifetime love of reading starts with a single step!

©2022 The LEGO Group and Universal City Studios LLC and Amblin Entertainment, Inc. All rights reserved. LEGO, the LEGO logo, the Brick and Knob configurations and the Minifigure are trademarks and/or copyrights of the LEGO Group.

 Manufactured under license granted to AMEET Sp. z o.o. by the LEGO Group.

AMEET Sp. z o.o.
Nowe Sady 6, 94–102 Łódź—Poland
ameet@ameet.eu
www.ameet.eu

www.LEGO.com

Published in the United States by Random House Children's Books, a division of Penguin Random House LLC, 1745 Broadway, New York, NY 10019, and in Canada by Penguin Random House Canada Limited, Toronto.

Step into Reading, Random House, and the Random House colophon are registered trademarks of Penguin Random House LLC.

Visit us on the Web!
StepIntoReading.com
rhcbooks.com

Educators and librarians, for a variety of teaching tools, visit us at RHTeachersLibrarians.com

ISBN 978-0-593-38184-7 (trade)

MANUFACTURED IN CHINA
10 9 8 7 6 5 4 3 2

STEP INTO READING®

DARING DINOSAUR ADVENTURES!

A Collection of Five
Step 3 Early Readers

Random House 🏠 New York

CONTENTS

LEGO® JURASSIC WORLD

DRONE DELIVERY

based on the story by Maciej Andrysiak

illustrated by AMEET Studio

Random House 🏠 New York

Jurassic World was a wonderful theme park filled with dinosaurs on the island of Isla Nublar.

Vic Hoskins, the chief of security,
Claire Dearing, the park manager,
and Owen Grady, the raptor trainer,
were people who worked on the island.

They were flying around on drones
to make sure everything was okay.

Unfortunately, their boss,
Simon Masrani, liked surprises.
They saw him giving a speech
to a crowd.

"Uh-oh," Owen said.

They agreed that this

could not be good.

Mr. Masrani pulled the covers
off the cages behind him.
There was a blue *Allosaurus*
and a gray *T. rex*!

As soon as the carnivores
saw each other, they started
roaring and clawing
at their cages!

The dinosaurs escaped their cages!
They chased Mr. Masrani
and the other people.

"Looks like the dinosaurs
think it's lunchtime!"
Claire shouted.

The *Allosaurus* tried
to eat Mr. Masrani!

But Owen saved his boss

with the drone's tow cable.

The *T. rex* and the *Allosaurus*
stomped up Main Street.
Tourists screamed
and ran.

"Let's get to the food storehouse," said Claire.
"I know what you are thinking," Owen replied.

The team tied turkeys

to their tow cables

and raced back on their drones.

The *Allosaurus* and the *T. rex* chased the flying turkeys!

The hungry dinosaurs
roared and snapped
at the turkey.

They followed them

through the jungle . . .

. . . and right back into
their normal enclosures.
WHEW!

Everyone was safe,
and the dinosaurs got
their lunch.

Mr. Masrani ran up
to Owen and Claire
and thanked them for saving
him and the park guests.

"And it gives me another idea
for a park surprise," he said.

"You can do this every day!"
Mr. Masrani said as he
patted Owen on the back.
"The guests will love it!"

ROARING ROUNDUP

based on the story by Maciej Andrysiak
illustrated by AMEET Studio

Random House 🏠 New York

It was a beautiful day
at Jurassic World.

Even Owen Grady, the raptor trainer,

was getting a chance

to enjoy the afternoon.

Owen and his dog, Red,

often took the baby raptors

out on quiet days like this.

When Owen said, "Come on, girls,"
the four raptors, Blue, Charlie,
Delta, and Echo, looked up.

The little raptors seemed
nervous. They did not want
to get out of Owen's truck.

Suddenly, the ground rumbled
and shook. In the distance,
a herd of *Triceratops*
was coming their way!

Owen and Red jumped

back in the truck.

They raced ahead of the huge,

horned dinosaurs.

Owen jumped out of the truck

and onto the back of

a *Triceratops*.

Red and the raptors
followed him.

It was tough for Owen

to ride the big creature,

but he held on tight.

He rode the *Triceratops*
like it was a bull at the rodeo.

Owen hopped from one
Triceratops to another
until he reached the leader.

He tried to calm the leader,
but she could not be stopped.
She was leading the stampede
toward the Visitor Center!

The dinosaurs rumbled

down Main Street.

Blue stayed with Owen

while Red and the other raptors

herded some of the dinosaurs

down a side street.

Owen herded the rest

using the *Triceratops*'s horns

to steer!

They managed to get
the herd off Main Street
and back into the park.

In the distance, Owen

saw a baby *Triceratops*.

She was crying for her mother!

"Are you the cause
of all this trouble?"
Owen asked the baby
with a laugh.

The baby was so happy
to snuggle with her mother
once again.

Claire called Owen
on the walkie-talkie.
"Are you okay?"
she asked.
"Everything is fine,"
Owen replied.

"Good, because the guests loved the show. Mr. Masrani wants you to do it again this afternoon!" Claire said.

"Oh no!" Owen groaned.

"So much for

our peaceful day!"

TOUR TROUBLE

based on the story by Kurtis Lee Estes

illustrated by AMEET Studio

Random House 🏠 New York

Hudson Harper was a huge
Jurassic World fan.
When he broke the record
for the park's obstacle course,
he got a special surprise!

Simon Masrani, the park's owner,

was going to let Hudson

be the first person to try

the Tour Tracker 3000,

a virtual guide to Jurassic World!

Hudson was very excited.
He put on the headset
and started walking.
All he had to do was
follow the red bricks
through the park.

At the *T. rex* enclosure,
the Tour Tracker 3000
warned Hudson not to get
near the big red button.

But Hudson could not see

very well, and he bumped

right into the big red button.

Hudson kept walking.

He did not see the doors

of the *T. rex* enclosure open.

The *T. rex* was now free!

Next, the Tour Tracker 3000
led Hudson to Main Street,
where he got some ice cream.
Yum!

The other guests screamed
and ran when they saw
the *T. rex* that followed Hudson.

The *T. rex* caused a gyrosphere
to spin out of control.
The big ball rolled toward
the *Brachiosaurus* enclosure.

The gyrosphere smashed into
the wall of the enclosure.
Now the long-necked *Brachiosauruses*
and the *T. rex* were free.

Hudson continued to follow
the red bricks,
and the *Brachiosauruses*
followed him!

At the Aviary,
one of the *Brachiosauruses*
stumbled into a crane
and accidentally let
two *Pteranodons* free!

The *Pteranodons* swooped over

Hudson's head

without him noticing.

Hudson was a little disappointed.

He was not seeing any dinosaurs.

He decided to stop

and have a cookie.

Yum!

Meanwhile, the dinosaurs were roaming free in the park. The Asset Containment Unit, also known as the ACU, sprang into action!

The ACU team tried
to capture the *T. rex* as it roared
down Main Street.
They wanted to get it
away from the park's guests.

Another ACU team herded
the *Brachiosauruses.*

The dinosaurs were finally
back in the jungle.

Hudson was really disappointed.
He was not seeing any
dinosaurs. He decided
to head back.

He did not see any
of the action
going on behind him!

Hudson decided he would tell

Mr. Masrani that

the Tour Tracker 3000

was not very good.

If he had only looked up,

he would have seen

the ACU in action

with several dinosaurs

on the loose!

Because of the Tour Tracker 3000, Hudson even missed the ACU firing a net above his head to capture a flying *Pteranodon*!

Hudson was fed up

with the Tour Tracker 3000.

He could not see any dinosaurs

with it!

He hoped that Mr. Masrani

would not be upset

that he did not like

the new invention.

Mr. Masrani said that these things
take time to get right.
He offered Hudson
a dinosaur cookie in thanks. *Yum!*
At least the day was not
a complete loss.

STEP INTO READING®

OPERATION SURVIVAL

based on the story by Margaret Wang

illustrated by AMEET Studio

Random House 🏠 New York

Owen Grady and Claire Dearing

worked at Jurassic World,

a theme park filled

with live dinosaurs.

And where there were dinosaurs,
there was trouble.
The park's *Pteranodons*
were flying reptiles.
They were beautiful to see,
but hard to catch.

And at the moment, there were

Pteranodons flying free.

Vic Hoskins, the security director,

was getting the ACU,

the Asset Containment Unit,

ready to go catch them.

The ACU were about to
take flight in their
hover-drone vehicles.

The drones flew higher than the *Pteranodons*, but the flying reptiles were quicker.

The ACU dropped nets that the *Pteranodons* easily avoided.

One *Pteranodon* hit a drone,
and the pilot fell through the air.
He waited to pull his parachute
so his teammates could fire
sleeping darts at the dinosaurs.

"Hurry up, guys!" the pilot said.
"This *Pteranodon*

looks hungry!"

Mr. Masrani was yelling
at the ACU team. He wanted
to know what was going on.
Unfortunately, the *Pteranodons*
avoided the darts, and the pilots
hit each other!

Now they were sleepy!

Mr. Masrani, Owen, and Claire
saw it all from a watchtower.
The *Pteranodons* were
too much for the sleepy pilots.

Vic radioed them.
Things were not going
according to plan!

Claire had an idea.

Maybe they could make

the *Pteranodons* come to them!

She called the Jurassic World kitchen and told them to bring as much fish as they could find to the Aviary.

At the Aviary, Claire and Owen
scooped up the fish
and threw them into the air.
"Dinnertime!" Claire yelled.
The *Pteranodons*
returned to the Aviary
for the feast!

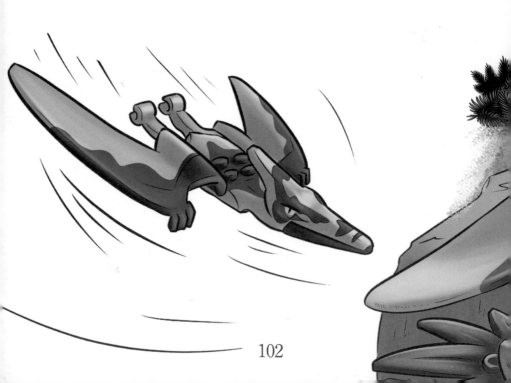

Soon the *Pteranodons*
became sleepy from eating
so much fish.
They settled down
for a long, quiet nap.

Owen gave the order
to close up the roof
of the Aviary.
Everyone cheered.

But the day wasn't over yet.

Guests at Jurassic World

were always coming and going.

And the park was a big place.

On Main Street, visitors

were everywhere.

One of these visitors

was up to no good.

Can you spot him?

After their morning with
the *Pteranodons*, Claire
and Owen had work to do.
"There's something very special
we need to pick up,"
Claire said, pointing to a map.

They did not know that
Sinjin Prescott,
the treasure hunter,
was listening in.

"I bet it is treasure,"
Sinjin said. He jumped
on a motorcycle and followed
Owen's truck.

But getting around
Jurassic World was not
as easy as he thought it
would be.

When a *Triceratops* blocked
his path in the swamp,
Sinjin yelled at it.
The large dinosaur swatted him
into the swamp.

Sinjin jumped just in time
to grab a vine
before his motorcycle
sank into the muck.

Sinjin decided that he had

enough time to stop

for a snack. But when he

pulled out his sandwich,

a bunch of *Compsognathuses*

came to investigate.

The dinosaurs were hungry,

and that sandwich looked good.

Sinjin threw it to them

and ran!

Sinjin was not looking
as he ran through the jungle.
He fell off a cliff and
into a *Pteranodon*'s nest.
From up in the nest,
he could see what Owen
was up to—Owen had
found a big egg.

Just then, the *Pteranodon*
knocked him out of her nest.
He plummeted
to the ground, landing
next to Owen's truck.
THUMP!
"This egg is a real
    treasure!" Claire said.
"Don't you agree, Sinjin?"

"No treasure is worth
coming back to *this* island,"
Sinjin said as they drove him
and the new egg
back to Jurassic World.
"There's always trouble."

PARK PROBLEMS

by Meredith Rusu

based on a screenplay by Jeremy Adams

illustrated by AMEET Studio

Random House 🏠 New York

All kinds of dinosaurs
roamed Isla Nublar,
the island home
of the famous park
Jurassic World!

Simon Masrani owned
Jurassic World. He had
gathered some of the employees
to tell them what a great job
they were doing and that they
should all relax.

Claire Dearing called Owen Grady

to relay the message to him.

Owen shook his head.

He knew that there was

always work to be done

on the island.

In fact, at that very moment,
Owen and his dog, Red,
were busy with some
new raptor eggs.

He delivered them
to the raptor enclosure
and told his favorite raptor,
Blue, to look after the eggs.

Vic Hoskins, the security director,
saw Owen and asked
how things were going.
"Those raptor eggs should
be fine until they hatch,"
Owen replied.

"You should learn to relax,"
Claire said as she walked up.
Owen shook his head.
There was always something
going on at Jurassic World.

Just then, Owen heard

a thunderous noise

and a cry for help.

A gyrosphere was caught

in a herd of

charging *Triceratops*.

Thinking fast,
Owen climbed down a vine
to the ground,
moving quickly past
a curious *T. rex*.
"Good girl. Good girl,"
Owen said.

When he reached the ground,

he ran through the herd

and pushed the gyrosphere

to safety.

"Thanks, Owen," the driver said.

"I don't know what we

would do without you."

There would be no rest
for Owen. In another part
of the park, Danny Nedermeyer
was up to no good.

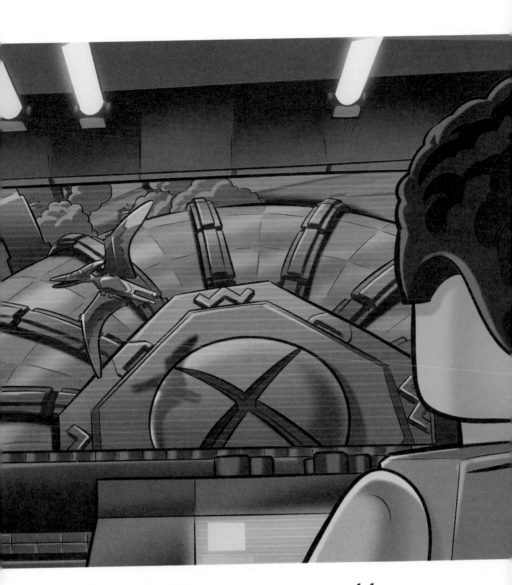

Danny liked to cause trouble.

He had decided to see what

would happen if he let

a *Pteranodon* loose.

Hearing that a *Pteranodon*
had been freed
from the Aviary,
Vic and Owen jumped
into a helicopter
and flew after her.
"I think this requires
a more hands-on approach,"
Owen told Vic.
Then he jumped out
of the helicopter!

Owen grabbed on to
the flying reptile's back legs.
"I'll guide her back to
the Aviary!" Owen shouted.
"You follow."

Vic nodded

from the helicopter.

Owen was worried

that more would go wrong

at the park.

He and Claire decided
to go on patrol that night
in a truck.

At the *T. rex* enclosure,
everything was quiet.
The green light meant
that everything was
locked up tight.

Owen wanted to wait.

He watched the green light.

He had a bad feeling . . .

and he was right!

In the control room,
Danny decided
to unlock the door
to the *T. rex* enclosure.

With the door unlocked,
the *T. rex* was free.
It roared and charged
at the truck!

But Owen was ready
for the dinosaur.
He fired a cannon net.
BOOM!

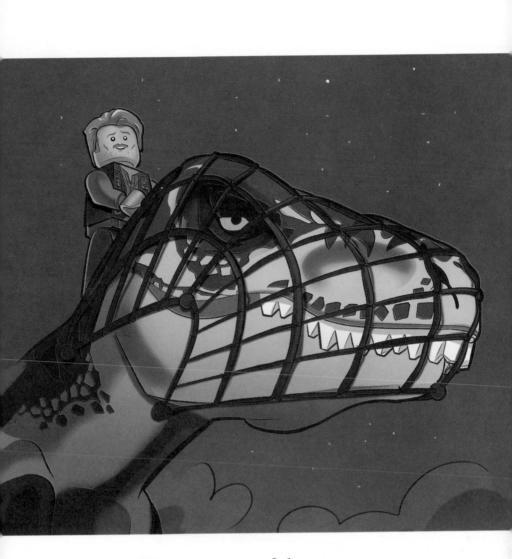

With a net safely over
her jaws, the *T. rex*
quieted down.
Owen led her back
into her pen.

Mr. Masrani knew Danny

was up to something.

"What are you doing?"

Mr. Masrani yelled.

Danny said he was keeping

the team on their toes.

"Excellent!" Mr. Masrani said.

Meanwhile, Owen and Claire
were happy the day
was over, but . . .

. . . as Owen always said, the work at Jurassic World was never over. He headed off with Blue to check on the raptor eggs.

THE DINOSAURS AND PEOPLE OF JURASSIC WORLD

PEOPLE AND COMPANIONS OF JURASSIC WORLD

Owen Grady: He is an animal behaviorist at Jurassic World. He is the trainer of a group of intelligent raptors named Blue, Charlie, Delta, and Echo. He and his canine companion, Red, are inseparable.

Red: Red is Owen Grady's lovable dog. He is ready for any adventure, even ones that require him to go snout to snout with big dinosaurs.

Claire Dearing: She is the Assistant Park Operations Manager at Jurassic World. She makes sure the park functions properly and that the guests are satisfied with their visit.

Simon Masrani: He is the billionaire owner of Jurassic World who never stops coming up with exciting new attractions for the park's guests.

Vic Hoskins: He is the security director at Jurassic World. Unlike Owen, he doesn't want to work with the dinosaurs. He thinks he can use his high-tech equipment to control them.

Danny Nedermeyer: Danny works for Jurassic World, but what he really likes doing is causing trouble. Luckily, Owen and Claire are there to keep the park safe.

Dr. Henry Wu: Dr. Wu is the scientist who makes all the dinosaurs at Jurassic World.

DINOSAURS OF JURASSIC WORLD

Tyrannosaurus rex (T. rex): This mighty, ferocious meat-eating predator, usually called T. rex, is Mr. Masrani's most impressive asset and the most popular attraction in the park.

Velociraptors: These small meat-eating dinosaurs are fast and intelligent. They hunt in packs and are best known for the sharp, curved claw they have on each foot.

Pteranodon: This flying reptile looks hungry and menacing. Luckily, her long beak is toothless and mostly used for catching fish.

Triceratops: This plant-eating dinosaur is built like a tank. Its long horns and neck frill give it plenty of protection when fighting predators like *T. rex*.

Stegosaurus: This plant-eating dinosaur is known for the plates on its back. It also has sharp spikes on its long tail.

Brachiosaurus: This dinosaur has a very long neck so that she can eat the leaves from tall trees.

THE END